Disney's DuckTales

The Road to Riches

A Golden Book · New York

Western Publishing Company, Inc., Racine, Wisconsin 53404

Scrooge McDuck was with his grandnephews, Huey, Dewey, and Louie, in his mansion on a hilltop in Duckburg. While looking at the roomful of treasures that he had brought back from around the world, he sighed.

"It's no use," he said. "There's no place left to go to search for new treasure. Let's face it, I'm through."

"Don't worry, Uncle Scrooge," said Huey. "We'll think of something. Now we've got to hurry, or we'll be late for our Junior Woodchucks meeting."

At the meeting the boys joined the other
Woodchucks around the campfire, where their
leader, the Grand Mogul, was telling a story.

"Long ago there was a tiny country in the
Himalaya Mountains near Tibet called the
Kingdom of Feathers. Its ruler, the Leader of the
Quack, collected a fortune in jewels in his Cave of
Splendor. Then everyone in the kingdom suddenly
vanished. Legend says that the fortune is still
there somewhere. It can be found by an explorer
who is daring enough."

"That treasure is just the thing to cheer up
Uncle Scrooge," said Dewey as they raced home.
But Scrooge wasn't there. The boys found him
sitting gloomily in the money bin down at his
office.

"We have the answer to your problem," Louie
said. "You're going to find the lost treasure of the
Kingdom of Feathers."

"You mean there's a treasure left that I hadn't
heard of?" said Scrooge. "Time's a-wasting!"

In a flash Scrooge and the boys were off to see Gyro Gearloose, the famous inventor.

Scrooge said, "We need a vehicle to take us to find the lost treasure of the Kingdom of Feathers. It must fly as fast as a jet, land in tight places like a helicopter, scale mountains, and float on water. And most important, it has to have room to hold treasure."

"This is a tough order," said Gyro. "It will take awhile. Come back in half an hour."

Next Scrooge and the boys went to see the fearless test pilot Launchpad McQuack.

"There isn't an aircraft that's been invented or will be invented that Launchpad can't fly," said Doofus, his sidekick and admirer. "And if Launchpad's going to fly it, I'm going to ride in it," he added.

At the next Junior Woodchucks meeting Huey,
Dewey, Louie, and Doofus told the Grand Mogul
about their trip.

"Uncle Scrooge said we could go along," said
Huey. "After all, if it weren't for us, there would be
no trip."

The boys were overheard by Quacker McFink, a
young duck paid by Flintheart Glomgold to spy on
them. Flintheart was so jealous of Scrooge that he
seized every chance to learn about his rival's
plans.

After making sure that there was nothing else to hear, Quacker McFink raced to Flintheart Glomgold's house and breathlessly told him about Scrooge's trip to the Kingdom of Feathers.

"We'll just see about that," said Flintheart. "I have some ideas of my own about getting that treasure."

In a few days Scrooge and his party were ready
to leave.

"Will you be needing your dinner jacket, sir?"
asked Scrooge's butler, Duckworth.

"We've organized an exploration party, not a
fancy-dress party," said Scrooge. "I'll need my
hiking boots."

As Launchpad began to take off, Scrooge's housekeeper, Mrs. Beakley, came running across the airstrip in her nightgown and slippers. When she couldn't find her granddaughter, Webbigail, she suspected the girl had stowed away on the plane.

"Webby!" she shouted. "Is my Webbigail in there?"

No one could hear her over the noise of the engine.

Doofus thought that Mrs. Beakley wanted to come along, so he opened the door and pulled her aboard just as they were taking off.

When Mrs. Beakley realized she was being lifted off the ground, she had no choice but to hold on. As she landed on the floor of the plane with a thud, she sat up, took one look around, and fainted.

"Grandma!" shouted Webby, coming out from behind a seat.

"Oh, *that's* what Mrs. Beakley was shouting about," said Doofus.

After Mrs. Beakley came to, everyone convinced her not to make them turn back. They even forgave Webby for having stowed away.

Launchpad flew the plane for a whole day without resting. Then he landed on a tiny plot of ground high in the Himalayas.

While looking at a map he said, "This is as far as we can fly. Now it's up to our feet."

As the crew left the plane they didn't know that Flintheart was spying on them. He had arrived by helicopter with the Beagle Boys, whom he had hired to lead a group of yaks.

"Just wait awhile," he told them. "Then we'll follow Scrooge's trail."

"We ought to be close to the Cave of Splendor, where the jewels are," said Scrooge as he and his band of adventurers set out along a mountain pass.

After a while, Scrooge said to Launchpad, "Are you sure you read the map right?"

Suddenly Huey, Dewey, and Louie went tumbling over a rock in the path and bumped into the side of a cliff. A huge stone door swung open. The explorers stood in the mouth of a very dark cave.

"Don't worry, Junior Woodchucks always carry flashlights," said Dewey.

Soon everyone was exploring the cave, heading down a long corridor that lead into a large cavern.

"Wow, Uncle Scrooge!" said Louie. "It's just the way the Grand Mogul said it would be."

Indeed the treasure was fabulous. The crew made their way past piles of jewels.

Rounding a corner, they stopped in their tracks. Before them stood the prize of the collection, the jewel-covered statue known as the Peeking Duck.

"Doesn't that statue remind you of someone?" asked Mrs. Beakley.

"Just hold it right there!" yelled a gruff voice from behind them.

Everyone whirled around to see Flintheart Glomgold and the Beagle Boys leading yaks.

After forcing Scrooge and his fellow explorers to
stand close together, Flintheart and the Beagle
Boys tied them up. Then they loaded all the
treasure onto the yaks until it looked as if the poor
beasts wouldn't be able to stand.

When the yaks were out of the cave, Mrs. Beakley
said, "I don't like the sound of that. I think they
are closing up the entrance to the cave!"

Indeed they were. Things looked bleak for Scrooge and his friends.

All of a sudden a small muffled voice piped up, "We're not licked yet, boys."

And then a small head peeked out from under Mrs. Beakley's nightgown.

"Webby!" everyone shouted.

Webby untied Mrs. Beakley, and they went to work untying the others.

Scrooge said glumly, "Now all we have to do is find a way out of here."

After trying in vain to get out of the cave, everyone was tired and gloomy.

Doofus said, "At least we've got the super-duper long-lasting food that Gyro packed along with us." And he took out two long, hard sticks. But he could neither bite them nor break them.

Scrooge said sadly, "I think we've had it."

Huey, Dewey, and Louie suddenly went into a huddle, then just as suddenly got up again. Louie grabbed two food sticks and ran to the cave door. Using one as a hammer and the other as a chisel, he began to dig through the rock.

"Hooray!" shouted Webby. "We're saved!"

It took awhile, but at last, with everyone's help,
there was an opening in the cave door large
enough to squeeze through.

"Now to stop Glomgold!" shouted Scrooge.

Everyone raced down the mountain path
toward the spot where they had landed. Flintheart
had brought his helicopter out of hiding and had
just finished loading the last piece of
treasure—the Peeking Duck—onto it.

"Stop!" shouted Scrooge.

Flintheart quickly slammed the helicopter door and took off. It looked as if he were going to get away. But then he peered over his shoulder to gloat at Scrooge—and bumped smack into the side of a mountain.

The door of the helicopter flew open, and out fell all the treasure. It scattered down the mountainside into a canyon so deep that no one could see the bottom.

Flintheart miraculously landed on a yak, unhurt. But he didn't look happy at having to face the angry, unpaid Beagle Boys. "Get me out of here!" he screamed to Scrooge.

Scrooge chuckled over Flintheart's fate. But as the airplane took off he looked sadly at the spot where the treasure had disappeared.

"Cheer up, Uncle Scrooge," said Huey. "There will be other treasures to find."

Scrooge was about to protest when he stopped. "Thanks to you three—and Webby—there will be. For, right now, you're all the treasure I need."